BLOOD & LEAVES

ONE MAN'S FIGHT AGAINST WILDLIFE TRAFFICKING

SAGE KANE

CONTENTS

CHAPTER 1: THE FOREST EDGE

GUNUNG LEUSER NATIONAL PARK—DAY 1, 10:00 AM

David Chen's last clear thought before the forest swallowed him: *three thousand dollars for this.*

One moment, sky. The next, green walls pressed in from every direction. The canopy closed overhead—a cathedral of chaos where sunlight filtered down in heavy, disorienting beams.

"Stay close," Rudi Santoso said, voice calm in the humid air. "Forest different from city. Easy to lose direction."

David Chen had been in Sumatra for exactly four hours. His expensive hiking boots—comfortable during training walks around Sydney's coastal paths—were already caked in mud. His camera gear—worth more than his guide earned in two years—caught on every vine.

Civilization was gone. Only dense green stretched ahead.

This had seemed like a good idea yesterday.

Bukit Lawang, North Sumatra – Day 1, 06.00 AM

. . .

They climbed into Rudi's Toyota pickup. Paint faded, seats patched with duct tape. This was no tourist prop, just a working truck for foreigners willing to go far.

"How long have you been guiding?" David asked as Rudi coaxed the engine to life.

"Five years guiding. My family from this land, long time. I know the forest—every tree, every path, every animal."

The casual confidence should have been reassuring. Instead, David noted the dropped articles and simplified grammar—signs of communication barriers he hadn't expected. Website reviews had been mixed: some raved about authenticity, others complained about unkept promises.

David had chosen Rudi based on price and availability rather than references, a decision Sarah would have questioned.

David was running from a failed marriage. Six months divorced from Sarah, who'd grown tired of waiting for him to choose her over the next assignment, the next escape dressed as work.

Now, watching the Sumatran forest blur past the truck windows, he wondered if she'd been right.

They drove through Bukit Lawang as the town woke— motorcycles threading between cars with suicidal precision, street vendors firing up carts in aromatic smoke that mixed engine exhaust with spices. The city gave way to palm oil plantations stretching toward the mountains, endless rows of identical trees tightening David's chest with claustrophobia and moral horror. Secondary forest appeared, and then, finally, the park entrance.

Registration was brief: forms in Bahasa, arbitrary fees, and quick warnings he barely understood. The rangers looked capable but exhausted.

"Trail difficult today," Rudi explained as they shouldered packs and prepared to enter terrain that would test every assumption David had made about his own preparedness. "Rain last night makes ground slippery. Leeches everywhere. River high from the mountain. We go slow, be careful."

David checked his camera straps, testing the balance between safety and speed. Miss the moment, miss the shot.

David's phone buzzed in his pocket.

Cloud Backup Complete: 3 photos uploaded
Location: Bukit Lawang, North Sumatra
Timestamp: 06:24 AM

Rudi noticed. "You photograph everything?"

"Habit. Automatic backup system." David showed him the notification. "Lost an entire month of work in Antarctica to a corrupted memory card. Never again."

"That thing kill your battery in forest. No signal anyway."

"Probably." David pocketed the phone, not mentioning that the system uploaded whenever a signal was available, whether he triggered it or not. Marcus complained about the notifications constantly, but paranoia had proven useful before.

The forest edge loomed—a wall of green. Rudi moved toward it, calm and casual.

"You ready?" Rudi asked, adjusting his minimal pack with movements that suggested this was routine rather than an adventure.

David nodded, though he didn't feel ready; the forest played by rules he didn't know.

～

Gunung Leuser National Park—Day 1, 10:00 AM

· · ·

The forest hadn't changed, but David had. Every step felt heavier now, every sound sharper, every shadow more suspicious. He adjusted his pack and followed Rudi deeper into the green, already aware that the jungle played by rules he had yet to learn.

Humid air wrapped everything in fog. David struggled to breathe. His shirt, meant to keep him dry, clung to his skin. Every step was a fight.

Bird calls echoed from everywhere and nowhere; insects hummed in alien rhythms. Water dripped from leaves in arrhythmic percussion, scrambling his sense of direction within minutes.

The path vanished and reappeared unpredictably; roots, vines, and fallen logs turned each step into a calculated challenge. Every step demanded balance and focus; the mental effort drained him faster than his body alone could sustain.

Movement in the canopy. Something large swinging between branches with fluid grace.

"Orangutan?" David raised his camera, trying to track it through the vegetation.

"Langur." Rudi didn't even look up. "Good practice, though. Follow the movement."

David photographed the monkey anyway, learning how his equipment handled motion in dense vegetation and discovering that forest photography required skills different from those of any other environment he'd worked in. The animal seemed curious about their presence, following them for several minutes with intelligent black eyes before disappearing into the undergrowth that might as well have been another dimension.

The trail climbed. David's gym fitness meant nothing. His heart pounded, sweat poured off him, and salt crusted on his skin. The air was thick and heavy; every breath was work.

"Need rest?" Rudi asked after ninety minutes, noting David's labored breathing with the assessment of someone who'd dealt with overheated clients before.

David wanted to say no, to prove he was prepared. But his

body decided. He needed to stop before he collapsed. Pride meant less than survival.

They stopped in a clearing where actual sky appeared overhead—startlingly blue after the green twilight that had enclosed them for the past hour. The sudden openness felt disorienting after the constant compression of vegetation.

David pulled out water and a bar, his hands shaking. Rudi ate rice wrapped in banana leaf—so much better for this place than David's imported snacks.

"How much farther to the orangutan area?" David asked, though he suspected the question might be pointless in an environment where animals moved according to their own schedules rather than human expectations.

"Depend on terrain, weather, luck with animal movement." Rudi's tone lacked the confident certainty of that morning's departure. "Forest very big, orangutan very smart. They move where they want, when they want. We can follow, but cannot control."

David watched Rudi's face as he spoke. The casual expertise from the guesthouse had become educated guessing. His guide had cultural context for forest survival and extensive local knowledge, but they were both operating in circumstances that required adaptation rather than the simple application of established procedures.

They walked on. The trail faded with each passing hour.

David's sense of direction failed; every direction looked the same—the forest closing around them like a fist.

"Do you actually know where we are?" David asked quietly after another forty minutes of uncertain progress.

Rudi stopped, staring at his phone. The screen was blank—no signal, no data, just the blue dot floating in empty space.

"Forest very big," he said, trying to hide his worry. "GPS no good here."

"So we're lost," David said.

"Not lost. Just... not sure where we are." Rudi tried to sound certain. "We find stream, follow downstream. Water goes somewhere."

The forest hummed, indifferent to them. It was beautiful, but pressed close. What promised adventure now delivered only confusion.

David's expensive adventure had become something else. It was testing skills he'd never needed and showing him limits he'd never met.

The forest remained silent. And somewhere in that silence, something was waiting.

CHAPTER 2: RUNNING TOWARD OR AWAY

Sydney, Australia—Three weeks before departure

Three weeks earlier, the forest hadn't yet claimed him. But something else already had.

Sarah moved through the Paddington terrace with practiced stillness, dark hair tied in her work bun. Tape ripped; pale rectangles marked where pictures had hung.

"You don't have to watch."

"I keep trying to say something wise. Like there's a sentence that can explain eight years."

She paused over a photo from Uluru—two people once sure love solved more than it complicated. She'd laughed at something stupid he'd said about the light, something about god's aperture or photographer nonsense. He couldn't remember the joke now, only that her laugh had made him believe he could be the person she saw when she looked at him."Maybe there's nothing left to say."

He gestured at the space where her drafting table had been. "I'm still going to Sumatra."

"Of course you are. You picked Iceland over Fiji for our

honeymoon and called it destiny. Every assignment was more important than us."

"You hate camping."

"You never asked." She closed the box. "That's what I hate."

She left. The door thudded. The house went hollow.

Outside, Mrs. Patterson watered her lavender, steady as always. He used to pity her routine. Now he wondered what it had saved her from.

His phone vibrated.

Final payment reminder.

He hesitated, not because of the money, but because part of him wanted the universe to intervene—an error message, an expired card, anything to make the decision for him. But nothing did. He transferred the money.

The confirmation blinked back at him. In the dark screen, his reflection layered over the empty room—rectangles where frames had hung.

Evidence stayed; meaning didn't.

The phone rang.

John, his editor at *Geographic Australia*.

"Perfect timing," John said. "I've got something for next issue —Great Barrier Reef, coral restoration with Dr. Rebecca Jones. Peak spawning light. It's your shot."

Six months ago, David would have said yes before John finished the sentence. But the confirmation email for Sumatra still glowed in the corner of his screen, waiting like a witness.

"When do you need me?"

"Next month. Funding's solid. It's important, David—and it pays."

"I can't," he said. "I'm committed to something else."

"Indonesia thing? I thought that was personal work."

"It is."

"David, I've worked with you for six years. You don't turn down paying assignments for personal projects."

"Maybe I'm learning to follow through."

John paused. "You once rescheduled your honeymoon to shoot a volcano."

He could still feel the ash in his lungs, and the silence that followed.

"Maybe I shouldn't have," he said.

Another pause—longer this time. "Your call," John said. "Keep me posted if you come to your senses."

The line clicked. The room was quiet again, and for the first time, that quiet didn't feel like peace.

He walked through the house—the map wall with pinholes like sutures, the floorboard that always complained, the patio where tomatoes failed and possums thrived. Everything that had been theirs was now just his.

His phone lit again. Not Sarah. A reminder: *renew travel insurance*. He opened a blank note and typed, *Running toward or away?* He didn't answer.

He called his mother in Perth. Margaret answered on the second ring, the sounds of her kitchen soft in the background— tap on, tap off, spoon set down.

"I'm having second thoughts," he said.

"About the expense?" Practical concern, not suspicion.

"About everything. Sarah thinks I'm running away."

"Why are you going?" she asked. "The real reason. Not the one for the magazine."

He considered the practiced answers—conservation, awareness, art as witness—and then said the only honest thing left.

"I don't know who I am without the marriage. I don't know if the person I built is worth keeping."

"And Sumatra will answer that?"

"Maybe it'll just postpone the question while I take expensive photos."

"When your father and I chased our dreams, we knew the difference between sacrifice and escape," she said. Her voice carried the weight of someone who'd raised a son alone after a heart attack took his father at forty-two. "We were building something together. The question isn't the cost, David—it's whether you're going toward something or away from it."

He closed his eyes. The house hummed—refrigerator, settling pipe, the city moving around his small complaint. "What if I don't know?"

"Then go find out. But be honest about what you find," she said. "Call me when you land."

They hung up.

The question stayed, echoing in the quiet apartment: *running toward or away?*

Outside, a bus sighed to a stop. He pictured strangers stepping off into the day they'd intend to have and the day they'd get.

He packed methodically—the way he always did before a trip. Cameras, lenses, batteries, and a cleaning kit, lined in military precision. From the right distance, it looked like bravery.

At the bedroom door, he paused where the bed had been. A square of carpet pressed flat. He sat in the space, trying to measure absence.

When light shifted and thinned to amber, he made coffee he didn't drink. The house held a quiet that made clocks sound arrogant.

That night, he took the framed Uluru photo from the box Sarah had left, looked at the strangers inside it, and sealed it away again.

He slept badly. Dreams stacked like luggage in a hallway—too heavy to lift, too in the way to ignore. He woke to the beginning of birds.

He showered and dressed in the same clothes he wore for every long flight. Checked cameras, backups, and batteries. Paranoia disguised as preparation.

He opened his laptop. The itinerary blinked: *Sydney–Kuala Lumpur–Medan. Pickup arranged. Contact: Rudi Santoso.*

He wrote to his mother: *Boarding this morning. Will text when I land. Love you.*

He wrote nothing to Sarah. Practiced writing her name, then deleted even that.

He zipped the duffel. The sound was the only thing left to say. Keys on the counter. Lights off. He stood in the doorway, hand on the frame—the same pose he'd taken a thousand times coming home.

He heard her voice again, not as accusation but as compass: *When will you risk something that truly matters?*

He locked the door.

The taxi idled in the street. "Airport?" the driver asked.

"Yeah," David said. "Airport."

They drove through a city not yet awake. Places they'd inhabited slid past—the corner shop with the crooked lottery sign, the fig tree that buckled the footpath. He catalogued them out of habit, as if turning the familiar into images could stop it from becoming history.

At the terminal, he joined the slow shuffle through security. Cameras in gray trays like offerings. There were easier ways to surrender.

At the gate, he wrote one more line in his notebook: *Running toward or away?* He still didn't answer.

The PA crackled. His destination came in a neutral voice.

He boarded with the others who believed they were in a hurry.

The city peeled away as squares of light. The coastline turned to line. The east lifted.

He closed his eyes. The engines drowned the part of the brain that made excuses.

In Medan, a guide named Rudi Santoso waited. Neither man knew yet what they would cost each other—or what they would save.

Above the clouds, the world was white and silent—the kind of silence he would soon learn to fear.

CHAPTER 3: DEEPER INTO THE FOREST

Gunung Leuser National Park—Day 1, 11:30 AM

They pushed deeper into the forest. With each step, certainty faded and unease crept in.

Rudi swung his machete at the vines. The casual confidence from this morning was gone. Each chop came careful now, measured. The blade rang sharp in the silence. Sweat ran down his neck. The silence between them grew heavier with every step.

David watched Rudi's back, something twisting beneath his ribs. *Three grand for this?* He bit the thought back—blame could wait. Right now, they just needed to get out.

Still, resentment sat low in his gut, keeping time with the throb in his leg. He tried to ignore it, focusing on the ground ahead.

Humidity wrapped him in a damp film. Sweat pooled under his shirt, salt crusting his arms. When he lifted his nearly empty water bottle, the plastic crinkled in his hand—a slight, sharp sound in the endless green.

He kept finding leeches. Five pulled from his calves so far, each leaving blood that wouldn't stop—the anticoagulant doing its work even after the creature was gone. He wiped them away and kept moving, but every stop cost time and a little more resolve.

David knelt to check the worst bite. The wound was swollen and hot, red streaks crawling up his shin. Pressure sent a pulse of pain deep into his bones. He winced and pulled his sock back up, pretending it didn't matter.

"Infection?" Rudi asked, noticing.

"Not yet. But infection's fast here." He pulled up his sock, glancing at Rudi. They had no antibiotics. The nearest clinic was at least a day away—if they could even find it. The thought hung between them, unspoken but heavy.

"How much farther?" David asked.

"Don't know," Rudi said, eyes averted.

The truth was worse than a lie. David wanted comfort, even if it was fake. All he got was honesty, sharp and cold.

They walked on. The forest seemed to close in, branches snagging David's camera, roots grabbing his ankles. Vines wove barriers behind them, closing every path but forward.

That Y-shaped tree—had they passed it already?

David checked his GPS. The blue line said 'forward.' The trees disagreed. They could walk in circles forever and never know.

"Have we been here before?" David asked, staring at the tree.

Rudi glanced at the trunk. "Maybe. All trees look same." He shrugged, already turning away.

Every direction looked the same. The forest closed around them, fingers tightening. No escape.

David knew this was paranoia, knew his exhausted brain was seeking patterns in chaos. But knowing it was irrational didn't make the feeling disappear.

The canopy overhead formed a lid, filtering sunlight in ways that made direction meaningless. Down here, in the cathedral of green, forward might be sideways, or backward, or in the same place as an hour ago.

His trail rations were nearly gone. He'd eaten the last energy bar for lunch, splitting it with Rudi in portions that satisfied neither. Dehydration dulled his thoughts. Every step dragged.

"We need water," David said, voice flat.

"Stream maybe one hour ahead." Rudi rechecked his phone—still no signal. "I hear water. We follow sound."

The logic was sound—water flowed downhill, downhill reached valleys, valleys held villages. That was the theory, anyway.

But nothing about this place was simple.

David nodded. No better plan. "Lead the way."

Rudi studied him for a moment, as if sensing the unspoken resentment beneath the practical cooperation. But he said nothing; he just turned and resumed cutting through the vegetation.

They walked in silence. David stared at Rudi's back. *This is your fault*, he thought. *You got us lost.* Then he crushed the thought and focused on placing one foot in front of the other.

Solutions, not blame. Get out—don't look back. He repeated it, hoping it would stick.

The forest changed. Fewer bird calls. Insects quieter. Even the water seemed to drip less frequently. David couldn't name what was wrong, only that something was.

The trees seemed to lean in closer, their trunks forming walls that funneled them through specific gaps. Clearings vanished as they neared. Every path ahead dissolved into thorns.

The forest was herding them. Dread, not logic, told David this.

His camera gear dragged him down—expensive anchors. Letting go would mean giving up on himself. He carried the weight anyway.

David's infected leg throbbed with each step. The red inflammation had spread slightly, creeping up his calf, suggesting the bacteria were winning. He tried not to think about sepsis, about organ failure, about dying in this forest because of a leech bite that should have been trivial.

"Stop," Rudi said, hand up, eyes narrowed.

David froze. The forest hummed. Then—a new sound.

Running water, somewhere ahead. The sound was a small promise, almost hopeful in the gloom.

Relief should have flooded through him. Instead, unease settled deeper. The forest had let them find this. After hours of keeping them circling through identical terrain, why did the forest offer them a stream now?

You're being paranoid, David told himself. *It's just a matter of geography, not a conspiracy.*

Still, every blocked path, every moment of confusion, felt like a nudge toward this stream—toward something unseen.

They pushed through the final screen of vegetation and emerged beside a stream wider and faster than expected. Brown water carried mountain runoff with enough force to be dangerous, rushing over rocks that would make crossing treacherous. The current looked strong enough to sweep away anyone who lost their footing.

"We follow downstream," Rudi said with obvious relief. "Water leads to villages eventually."

David studied the stream's curve, uneasy despite its ordinary look. Trees leaned in from both sides, forming a living corridor. There was no escape from the water's path now unless they wanted to battle thorns and shadows.

The stream was a road. The forest had built it for them.

But where did it lead?

David's phone buzzed with an unexpected signal—one bar appearing briefly like a taunt. He fumbled for it, typed with shaking hands: "Lost in forest need help" and hit send before the bar vanished.

Message failed.

Who would answer, even if it went through? Sarah, who'd called him a runner? John, who'd offered the safe path? His mother, who'd wanted to know if he was running toward or away.

He was away. So far away that "back" had stopped meaning anything.

"Who you message?" Rudi asked, voice quieter than before.

"No one. Signal died." David let the phone drop into his pocket.

"Tour company expects us tomorrow," Rudi said. "If we don't come back, maybe they look. But forest is big."

The implications were clear. In thousands of square kilometers of wilderness, rescue teams would never find two lost hikers who'd deliberately gone off established routes. They were invisible to any search efforts that might eventually be mounted.

They were on their own.

Rudi found a long branch and probed the stream systematically, mapping depths that varied from ankle-deep shallows to holes requiring swimming. The crossing would be possible, but it would be dangerous.

"We no cross now," Rudi decided. "Too risky with equipment. We follow bank, find safer place downstream."

David nodded, relieved despite himself. The thought of crossing that current while carrying camera gear had filled him with dread that went beyond rational assessment of danger.

They followed the stream. Hope was all they had. The banks were slick. Every step risked a fall.

As the afternoon shadows lengthened through the canopy, creating patterns of light and darkness that altered the forest's character, David felt the temperature begin to drop. Not much— maybe a degree or two—but enough to suggest evening was approaching faster than he'd anticipated.

They needed to make camp before dark, but neither wanted to stop. The stream was hope and direction. Abandoning it felt like giving up momentum they might never get back.

"You smell that?" Rudi's voice cut through the gloom, sharp and alert.

David inhaled. Beneath the rot—smoke. Not wood, but something chemical: diesel, plastic.

"Someone nearby?" Hope flared despite exhaustion.

"Maybe." Rudi's expression suggested he was considering

possibilities David didn't want to examine. "We follow stream. See what we find."

The smoke smell faded, but the wrongness remained. Something about the forest had shifted in ways David couldn't articulate. The bird calls had changed. The insects seemed to avoid certain areas. The vegetation showed gaps that might have been paths or evidence that people had passed this way.

They were walking toward something. The question was whether it would save them or worsen their situation.

David's expensive adventure had become more serious than he'd bargained for. The forest, promising authenticity, was delivering vulnerability—stripping away every assumption about competence and technological advantage.

Whatever answers he'd been seeking about authenticity and commitment, he was going to find them in circumstances that might not allow him to return and share what he'd learned.

The forest held secrets about survival that no amount of urban preparation could anticipate.

And somewhere downstream, following the muddy water through increasingly remote terrain, something waited that would transform their crisis from survival into a test of character neither man could have imagined.

David didn't know it yet, but the stream they'd committed to following was carrying them toward a discovery that would demand more than just their ability to stay alive. It would force them to choose who they were when nothing was left.

The real test was almost here. No safety net now, except courage—and each other.

CHAPTER 4: WHAT CAN'T BE UNSEEN

Day 2, 8:00 AM–Following the stream

Dawn arrived with a downpour. Rain drummed on the woven fronds above, pooling in curled leaves and bleeding through gaps. Every cold drip found David's spine. Their shelter sagged like a lung emptied of breath.

They'd spent a night hunched beside the stream, shivering in wet clothes. David winced as he checked his leg—red streaks now snaked from the bite, angry lines crawling up his calf. His muscles ached and his skin felt tight, feverish heat radiating outward. Even his thoughts blurred at the edges. Fever logic, where everything connected and nothing made sense.

Rudi's jaw clenched as he packed up, his usual easy banter gone. When they finished the last of their water, he dipped bottles into the stream without a word. Purification tablets stayed in his pocket. Maybe it didn't matter anymore—sickness worried survivors, not the desperate.

Everything was soaked. David's camera case, supposedly waterproof, drooled muddy water when he set it down. His clothes plastered to his body, the ground so saturated it squelched under every movement.

"We need to find help," David said, his voice cracking. Each word hurt his throat.

Rudi studied the gray wall of vegetation ahead. "Which way?"

They'd lost orientation completely during the night. Phone compasses spun uselessly. The sky was a blank sheet of cloud.

They trudged along the stream, hope shrinking with every muddy bend. The jungle swallowed all hints of people: no cigarette butts, no chopped saplings, just endless green and the steady hush of water.

The animal path, if it could be called that, needed constant machete work. Rudi hacked at vines, his movements slow with exhaustion. David stumbled after him, his legs cramping with every step.

Then Rudi stopped. Held up his fist.

David froze. Listened.

Through the rain, through the constant forest sounds: voices. Human voices. Speaking rapid Indonesian.

Relief hit David like a punch. People. Rescue. Maybe hope.

They crept forward, branches brushing their faces. Rudi hunched, shoulders tight, his head darting side to side. Not relief now—caution, as if he could smell danger on the wet air.

A clearing opened ahead. Actual sky. The first they'd seen since entering the forest two days ago.

"People," David whispered, starting forward. "Thank God—"

Rudi grabbed his arm. Hard. His face had gone rigid.

David looked closer.

Blue plastic tarps covered rough wooden buildings. Vehicles sat under camouflage netting, clearly hidden on purpose, not just kept out of the rain.

And cages. Wooden cages arranged in rows, extending deeper into the clearing than David could count at first glance.

"What—"

Then he saw what was in the cages.

Orangutans.

Dozens of orangutans crowded the cages. Adults pressed their hands and faces to the bars, eyes following every movement with silent pleading. Young ones hunched in corners, ribs showing, knuckles gnawed raw. Babies—barely more than orange fuzz and frightened eyes—reached through gaps, fingers trembling, mewling softly for mothers who couldn't answer.

"Oh Jesus." The words came out as breath rather than voice.

Rudi was already pulling him down behind dense vegetation, his hand pressing David's shoulder with a pressure that demanded stillness. "Very quiet. These people very dangerous."

David couldn't move. Couldn't breathe. Couldn't process what he was seeing.

The babies broke him. Tiny wrists bore bruises from the bars. One stretched its hand toward David, palm out, fingers spread, eyes huge and wet. Another whimpered, a thin sound that belonged to something much smaller. A third rocked itself, searching for comfort that wasn't there.

Processing stations lined one edge of the clearing. There were plastic bins, tarps stained dark with substances David didn't want to identify, and equipment that suggested systematic butchery. Armed men moved between the structures with casual skill, their weapons and movements hinting at military training or experience in security.

This wasn't desperation. Inventory sheets hung on clipboards. The cages were numbered. Professional. Profitable. Industrial-scale extinction.

"Poaching operation," David whispered, the words inadequate for the horror they witnessed.

"We go," Rudi breathed, his voice carrying urgency that brooked no argument. "Now. Very quiet."

But David was already reaching for his camera. Years of professional work had trained his hands to act on instinct, even before he could think about the risks. This needed to be recorded.

Someone had to see what was happening in these forests, places most people would never visit.

"What you doing?" Rudi's voice was sharp with alarm. "They catch us, they kill us."

"Someone has to know."

David raised his camera, his hands shaking, but his finger still found the shutter with practiced precision. The lens brought the horror into sharp focus, every detail captured with the skill he had spent years developing.

Click. Baby orangutan, hand through bars.

Click. Processing station, evidence of systematic slaughter.

Click. Armed guard, assault rifle held with casual competence.

Click. Truck loaded with cages, license plate visible.

Looking through the camera, David saw that every detail was proof. Mothers and babies were kept apart by bars and cruelty. Bodies were taken apart quickly, like in a factory. Price tags on crates turned these animals into products, their lives reduced to numbers on a balance sheet.

This was the destruction of a whole species, carried out on a massive scale. The animals were already struggling to survive in the little habitat they had left.

David lowered his camera and pulled out his phone, his hands shaking. His professional gear might be taken, but phone photos, though lower in quality, had GPS data and would back up automatically when there was a signal. He always kept multiple copies on different devices, a habit he had kept since Antarctica.

Click-click-click. The phone's camera captured a dozen quick frames: the camp layout, the cages, the armed guards, the processing equipment. Each image was tagged with GPS coordinates and would wait for a signal to upload to cloud storage. Marcus would see the backup notifications and know something was wrong.

His phone buzzed once, searching for a signal. The canopy swallowed all but its futile attempt. It would keep trying and connect as soon as any coverage appeared.

He swapped the phone for the camera, steadied it, but the viewfinder showed too much like a reflection.

He clicked twice. Then lowered it.

Light.

A shaft of morning sun broke through clouds, hit his camera lens at exactly the wrong angle.

The glint bounced straight into the clearing, making it obvious that someone was watching and threatening the camp's security.

"Shit—"

A shout erupted from the camp. David didn't understand the Indonesian words, but their tone made the meaning clear: alarm, urgency, and threat.

"INTRUDERS! SECTOR THREE!"

Men were turning, looking their direction. Pointing. Reaching for weapons.

"Run," Rudi breathed. "Now."

But it was too late.

Voices exploded across the clearing. Orders shouted in Indonesian with military precision. Boots on wet ground converged on their position.

David looked at Rudi. Rudi's face had drained of color.

"How many?"

"Too many." Rudi was already moving, crouched low. "We run, maybe we make forest edge before—"

A man appeared through the vegetation. Twenty meters away. Assault rifle raised with competence, suggesting extensive training.

He saw them.

His eyes widened. Then his mouth opened—

"INTRUDERS! SECTOR THREE!"

The camp exploded into motion. Men running from multiple directions. Voices coordinating pursuit with military efficiency.

"RUN!" Rudi grabbed David's arm.

They ran.

Behind them, the sound of pursuit grew louder. It was professional, organized, and closing in quickly, the work of people who had done this before.

The forest had almost killed them through indifference.

Now it was their only hope.

David ran, gear thumping against his spine, breath tearing at his chest. His wounded leg sent up flares of pain that nearly blinded him. Sweat stung his eyes, and the air tasted thick as blood. His body begged to stop, but fear and the memory of the baby's reaching hand forced him forward.

Behind them: shouts, crashes, the methodical sound of trained men who knew how to hunt humans in terrain they controlled.

Ahead was a green maze with no exit. The forest that had kept them lost for two days was now their only hope of escape.

Rudi slashed through the brush, urgency in every swing. David stumbled after, his legs heavy as logs, mind swimming. He tried to command his body but felt it slipping, like shouting through water.

He stumbled.

Caught himself on a tree trunk.

Stumbled again.

His phone, still in his pocket from taking backup photos and still trying to upload images to the cloud, slipped free as he crashed through the undergrowth. It tumbled into the leaf litter with a soft thud. He didn't hear over his own gasping breaths and the sounds of pursuit getting closer.

The device landed face down in the decomposing vegetation. Its GPS was still active, the upload queue still waiting, and the backup system still working as designed, even as it vanished beneath the forest debris.

David didn't notice. Didn't register the weight missing from his pocket. His entire focus narrowed to the single task of staying upright, staying ahead of men with weapons, staying alive for the next thirty seconds because thinking further ahead was impossible.

The chase ended not with a gunshot, but with David's legs buckling. He tripped on a root, sprawling in the mud, camera gear tumbling in every direction. The equipment—the price of so many ambitions—lay splattered and useless, like the rest of his plans.

Lenses rolled away into the underbrush. Camera bodies hit the ground hard enough to crack their protective cases. Memory cards vanished into the leaf litter. His equipment was scattered across the forest floor, a wreckage of misplaced confidence.

Rudi could have escaped. His local knowledge and forest skills would have allowed him to disappear into vegetation, to confound pursuers, to vanish into a three-dimensional landscape where he held every advantage except numbers and firepower.

Rudi dropped to his knees beside David, scooping cameras from the mud. David blinked, throat tight—loyalty, not calculation, kept his friend here. Shame burned hotter than the fever for a moment.

"Go," David gasped, struggling to stand on legs shaking with exhaustion and infection. "Run. Save yourself."

"We stay together," Rudi said firmly, his voice carrying determination that seemed to come from principles deeper than practical calculation. "Both escape or both captured. Not leave friend behind."

The decision sealed their fate, bringing a sense of inevitability and tragedy. Within seconds, armed men emerged from the surrounding vegetation. Five professionals with military-grade weapons moved with tactical precision, surrounding their targets and keeping their weapons ready.

David raised his hands slowly, his camera strap still around his neck, marking him as an intruder. The equipment that once seemed so important was now just a useless burden, showing he had documented what they were doing.

The lead captor was older than the others, his scars showing years of violence. He had the calm authority of someone used to making life-and-death decisions without emotion. He looked at David's expensive equipment with a calculating gaze, assessing its value rather than admiring its quality.

"Cameras," the man said in accented English, gesturing for David to remove his gear.

David hesitated, knowing that giving up his equipment meant losing the evidence of what he had seen. The photographs were proof of crimes that law enforcement had been seeking for years. Without them, the orangutans would stay invisible to the outside world.

But the guard behind him pressed the rifle barrel into David's back, making his intentions clear. Any resistance would be met with swift and brutal consequences.

David slowly took off his cameras and handed them over, watching his professional life disappear into hostile hands. The lead captor looked over the gear, clearly appreciating its quality and value, before giving it to a subordinate for safekeeping and later inspection.

"You photograph our work?" the man asked, his English careful but precise.

David considered lying, claiming he was just a lost tourist who'd stumbled onto their operation by accident. But the camera lens and professional camera bodies made such deception pointless.

"Wildlife photography," David said finally. "I got lost looking for orangutans."

The man's laugh was genuinely amused, suggesting appreciation for irony rather than hostility toward deception. "Yes, you find orangutans. Too many orangutans, maybe. More than tourists should see."

They were marched back to the camp at gunpoint. David struggled to keep up on his infected leg, trying to process the full horror of what he saw up close. The operation was even larger than he had realized: processing stations for systematic slaughter, vehicle maintenance areas that suggested a permanent base, and communications equipment linking them to networks in several countries.

Dozens of cages held animals destined for international black markets, their lives ending to serve human greed on an industrial scale. The sound that would haunt David forever was the crying of baby orangutans, calling for mothers who could never answer. Their small voices created a heartbreaking chorus that showed their intelligence and emotional depth, demanding compassion.

The babies pressed their fingers through the bars. Their eyes searched David's face for hope. Some rocked, some whimpered. Some looked away. No more hope left to give.

They were shoved into a wooden cage barely large enough for two people to sit upright. It was built just like the cages for the orangutans, made from forest materials and tied with rope, traditional craftsmanship turned to criminal use.

The irony wasn't lost on David: seeking authentic experience in Sumatran forests, he found the most authentic expression of human cruelty and greed.

The cage was crude but effective, meant to hold creatures without the tools or knowledge to escape. The wooden bars were thick and close together, making it impossible to break or squeeze through, and the rope bindings were tight enough to prevent easy tampering.

Rudi sat beside him in the cramped space. Both men understood, even if they didn't say it out loud: their captors couldn't afford to leave witnesses. The evidence David had gathered threatened a network worth millions. Their deaths would be a business decision, not a crime of passion.

Through the gaps in the wooden walls, David watched the daily routine of the operation. Workers sorted animal parts with industrial efficiency. Guards patrolled with military discipline. Vehicles came and went with cargo David didn't want to think about.

But what caught his attention most were the orangutans in

the nearby cages, especially the babies who seemed to notice something different about their new neighbors. They pressed against the bars facing David and Rudi, making soft sounds that might have been attempts to communicate or just desperate efforts to reach out to anyone who showed kindness.

"They know we're different," David observed quietly.

"Animals understand more than people think," Rudi replied, his voice carrying sadness, suggesting personal experience with wildlife intelligence. "They know who wants to help and who wants to hurt."

As the afternoon shadows grew longer across the camp, David realized their situation gave them one terrible chance. If the criminals couldn't let witnesses live, maybe their last actions could still mean something.

The wooden cages were made to hold animals, not to stop humans from escaping. With enough time and stealth, someone who understood basic construction could make openings big enough for the small orangutans to get out.

Trying to help would be almost certain suicide. If they were caught, they would be killed immediately. But the only other option was to watch dozens of endangered animals die and do nothing.

David looked at Rudi and saw the same thoughts in his guide's eyes. They would probably die either way. But they could choose whether their deaths meant something more than just being silenced as witnesses.

For the first time since his marriage ended, David faced a choice that would show who he truly was, not just who he wanted to seem to be.

And whatever he decided would show if Sarah's accusations were true: whether he was really unable to sacrifice for others, or if he had just never found anything worth giving up his comfort to protect.

CHAPTER 5: THE CAGE

DAY 2, 4:00 PM—THE PUNISHMENT CAGE

The interrogation began at dusk.

The scarred leader introduced himself as Harto. He pulled a folding chair to their cage and sat, movements unhurried. He checked his watch—casual, as though they were scheduled clients rather than captives. His demeanor hinted at a man accustomed to compartmentalizing—perhaps a father who read bedtime stories after a day of industrial-scale slaughter. He knew fear and time worked better than violence. To him, this was just procedure.

David's fever blurred his mind. His infected leg throbbed. Sweat soaked his clothes. Terror sharpened his focus. Each question mattered.

Who knew where they were? Who would notice they were missing? Did anyone have their location? Would someone come looking?

The questions showed how clever these criminals were. They weren't just thugs—they were businessmen who traded in lives.

"Tour company expects us back yesterday," Rudi said during a pause in questioning, his voice carrying exhaustion. "When we don't return, they start looking."

Harto's smile was practiced. "Many tourists get lost in forest. Dangerous place. Sometimes we find bodies. Sometimes, nothing."

The threat was casual, more chilling for its calm. Killing witnesses was just business here.

"Need antibiotics," David said, showing his leg. Infection could kill him before they did.

"Maybe we get medicine," Harto said, voice flat. "Depends how helpful you are."

David knew helping only bought time. No promise would save them. This network couldn't leave witnesses.

Harto turned on David's cameras. His face darkened as he scrolled through photo after photo. Evidence that could ruin everything.

"Fifty-six photos," Harto said. "GPS data. You cost us money. You make us look weak."

He spoke rapidly in Indonesian to subordinates. David caught enough tone to understand they were discussing punishment options rather than simple execution.

After twenty minutes, Harto stood. "We discuss what to do with you. Meanwhile, you think about how much trouble you cause. Think about whether your photos are worth dying for."

He left them in the cage as evening shadows lengthened across the camp.

The poaching operation kept going. The horror was worse for being routine. Not desperate crime—just business.

Workers sorted animal parts at processing stations, their movements speaking of extensive practice. Guards patrolled in predictable patterns, maintaining the security perimeter with military discipline. Vehicles arrived and departed on schedules suggesting established supply chains connecting this remote location to markets demanding exotic materials.

Through gaps in their wooden cage, David watched the daily routine that treated extinction as an inventory management problem rather than a moral catastrophe.

But what caught his eye were the orangutans in their cages.

Dozens of them, arranged in rows that extended deeper into the camp than David had initially realized. Adults pressed against wooden bars with expressions showing intelligence, trapped by circumstances they couldn't control. Juveniles huddled together for comfort that captivity couldn't provide. Babies—some impossibly small—reached through gaps with tiny hands that seemed to be asking questions their captors would never answer.

The sounds were worse than the sights. Babies cried for mothers who never came. Adults cried for their young. Some made no sound at all—broken by cruelty.

In the cage adjacent to theirs, a baby orangutan—perhaps eighteen months old—pressed its face against the wooden bars, watching them with dark eyes that held more intelligence than many humans David had photographed. The young animal made soft sounds, not distress calls but something closer to communication attempts directed specifically at the two humans sharing its imprisonment.

The baby gripped the bars, small hands strong and clever. Its eyes tracked every movement, curious, not afraid—as if it knew these humans were different.

David watched the baby and felt something shift inside him—not pity, but a recognition of real intelligence and feeling. This was no ordinary animal. This was a being that could suffer, that understood its own captivity, that remembered freedom and mourned its loss.

Before the cage, the baby had known different arms—strong ones, orange-furred, that carried it through a canopy where sunlight flickered and danced. It had felt the slow heartbeat of safety, the warmth of a body that cared if it lived or died. Now, huddled behind bars, it pressed tiny fingers to wood—searching for a comfort it could only remember.

Now it would die here or in a private zoo. Its intelligence would mean nothing. It was just a number in a market that didn't care.

~

Evening came. The camp quieted. Rudi spoke about his daughters.

"My wife, Ratna," he said, staring at the darkening forest beyond their cage. "She worry when I guide tourists into deep forest. Say one day I not come back."

David heard the unspoken addition: *She was right.*

"Two daughters. Ayu is six, Sinta is four. Smart girls. They want to go to university someday." Rudi's voice carried the weight of dreams that might not survive his death. "My mother lives with us. Diabetes. Medicine costs more than I earn some months."

David had never had to do this math. For Rudi, every risk threatened his daughters' schooling, his wife's home, his mother's medicine. One slip, and everything would fall apart.

"If I die here," Rudi said, "Ratna takes the girls. My mother has no insulin. All of it—gone."

David wanted to reassure him but had nothing honest to offer. There were no comforting lies left.

"I'm sorry," David said. "This is my fault. I wanted wild orang-utans—off-trail—"

"We both made choices," Rudi said. "I took money, knowing risks. You paid, not knowing. Now we both pay the price."

They sat in silence, listening to the camp settle into evening routines. Guards changed shifts with military precision. Processing stations shut down for the night. The caged animals' distress calls diminished as darkness brought exhausted resignation rather than actual peace.

In the gathering dusk, David began to understand what Sarah had meant.

You photograph suffering from a distance and call it meaningful work. When will you actually risk something that truly matters?

He'd spent eight years documenting crises while maintaining careful distance from their consequences. Photographed poverty without confronting his own privilege. Documented environmental destruction without sacrificing his comfort to prevent it. Captured suffering through camera lenses that kept the pain safely removed from his own experience.

He'd mixed up awareness with real involvement, thought documenting was the same as committing, and believed observing from a distance could replace personal sacrifice.

But there was no distance now. Suffering pressed against bars, crying for mothers who would never come. The crisis was here, now—he was living it.

The choice wasn't comfortable anymore. It was brutal—did principle matter more than survival? Were some lives worth dying for?

Sarah had been right. He'd never risked what mattered. Never choose a principle when it costs more than time or money. Never found anything worth real sacrifice.

Until now.

"The rope bindings," David said, his eyes tracing every knot and loop of their cage. "Ours and the animal cages—are they built the same way?"

"Similar," Rudi said, running his fingers over the knots. "It's traditional hemp, twisted tight. Strong, but if you know pattern and have time, you can make it loose."

"How much time?"

Rudi studied the bindings, his hands sure from years of working with rope. "A few hours. Maybe all night, working slow. And only if the guards don't catch us during their rounds."

"But possible?"

"Yes. Possible."

David's mind snapped into focus. He watched the guards drift past, slow and careless, their routine stretched thin by confidence. Ninety minutes of darkness between each sweep—time enough, maybe, to pick at knots while the camp slept.

The baby orangutan in the next cage watched them, dark eyes following every gesture and whisper. Small hands curled tight around the bars—hands meant for swinging through branches, now wrapped around cold wood instead of open air.

"Even if we get out," David said, working through logical progression, "where do we go? We were lost before they caught us. Now we're deeper in the forest, farther from any rescue."

"Yes, but now we know where we are," Rudi said. "This camp needs supplies. Roads lead somewhere. That's better than wandering."

The logic was sound, but escape was just step one. They'd still need to cross a camp full of armed men, find a way out, and survive the forest.

Neither choice was easy. The other option was waiting for execution, doing nothing for the animals.

"The baby orangutans," David said, looking toward the nearest cage containing two juveniles pressed together for comfort. "Same rope construction?"

"Same rope, same knots, same weak spots," Rudi said, voice heavy. "But do we save ourselves, or them too?"

The moral choice was hard. Freeing orangutans meant risking everything, with a lower chance of survival. Any rational person would run and hope to find the rest.

But David thought about evidence. If he died rescuing animals, the photos would never reach anyone. Proof only worked if he survived.

But what he'd seen demanded action now, not later. Babies cried for their mothers. Butchery was routine. Cruelty was just business.

"How many could we realistically free?" David asked, moving beyond moral abstractions to practical planning.

"Maybe one, two cages maximum in the time we have," Rudi calculated with brutal honesty. "Guards patrol regular. We have maybe thirty minutes after we escape before someone notice. Wet rope comes apart faster—maybe five minutes per cage if we are fast. But rushing makes noise. Mistake brings guards."

David absorbed the mathematics. Thirty minutes. Maybe three babies would be freed if everything went perfectly. More likely two. Possibly none if they were discovered.

"We're probably going to die anyway," David said. "These people can't leave witnesses. The question is, do we die helping or die doing nothing?"

Rudi fell silent, his face tight with conflict. Practical survival warred with something deeper—principles that didn't fit into any easy calculation.

"My daughters," he said finally. "If I die trying to free animals, they grow up with no father. Ratna struggles alone. No medicine for mother's diabetes."

"I know."

"But my grandfather told me something." Rudi's voice carried the weight of wisdom transmitted across generations. "Seorang pemandu yang meninggalkan kliennya meninggalkan jiwa. A guide who abandons his client abandons his soul."

"I'm not your client anymore," David said. "We're just two people in the same terrible situation."

"Exactly." Rudi met his eyes. "So we're not guide and client. We're partners. And partners don't abandon each other. Don't abandon creatures who can't speak for themselves."

The decision was settled between them without requiring further discussion. They would attempt escape. They would try to free as many animals as they could reach in 30 minutes. They would probably die in the attempt. But at least they'd die choosing courage over comfort. Action over acceptance. Meaning over fear.

They started on the ropes as darkness settled over the camp.

Rudi showed David how to find tension in the ropes, how to work fibers loose without noise. The work took patience David never needed in city life.

At every approaching footstep, they went rigid, bodies slack against the cage floor, eyes pressed shut. Heartbeats thudded in the hush as boots crunched past. They waited, motionless, trading precious minutes for the illusion of helplessness.

David's leg made it hard to crouch. Pain fought his focus. Fever made every task harder.

But gradually, almost imperceptibly, the binding began to loosen. Individual fibers were separated from the weave. Knots worked free under repeated manipulation. The rope's strength faded, the fibers loosening just enough that a careful push could open a gap wide enough for someone to slip through—hidden weakness masked behind the knots.

The baby orangutan watched them, silent, face pressed to the bars. It seemed to know something was happening—and kept quiet.

The camp settled. Most guards left for their bunks. The cages fell quiet. Forest sounds rose outside—wild, alive, promising freedom.

"How long until morning?" David whispered, resting his cramped fingers.

"Maybe five hours," Rudi said, testing the rope. "Enough to open our cage. Then thirty minutes—no more—to free what we can."

The math was brutal. Even if all went well, they'd save a few while dozens stayed behind. But a few were better than none.

"The baby next to us," David said, looking at the young orangutan who'd been watching them all evening. "We free that one first."

"Agreed," Rudi said. "Then see how much time we have."

They worked at the ropes, fingers finding a rhythm in the

dark. The rope loosened with every pass. Hope grew with each strand.

Live or die, succeed or fail, David was finally risking everything for others—not just himself.

The rope loosened a little more with each pass of their hands. The baby orangutan watched in silent hope. In that darkness, David felt himself changing—becoming the kind of man who would risk everything for what truly mattered, not just for comfort or adventure.

No one was there to record it. The only witnesses were the animals whose futures hung on this quiet act of courage, freedom resting in the hands of people who had finally found something worth losing everything to protect.

The forest beyond the cage held freedom and danger. In six hours, they'd choose which one mattered more.

CHAPTER 6: THIRTY MINUTES TO MEANING

DAY 3, 3:00 AM—THIRTY MINUTES TO FREEDOM

Six hours for the rope to give. Wood scraped, fibers loosened. Finally, the bars parted just enough for a body. From across the camp, no one would notice.

"Ready?" Rudi whispered.

David nodded. Fever dulled every signal, leg pulsing with pain. Sweat glued his shirt to his back. Adrenaline surged, a shaky strength he knew could vanish at any second.

"Thirty minutes maximum," Rudi breathed. "Next patrol at three-thirty. We free what we can, then run for forest."

The bar creaked aside. David slid out first, bare feet sinking into soft, unfamiliar dirt. Rudi followed, silent as a shadow. They crouched by the empty cage, eyes flicking over the camp—every bulb, every path, every sound.

Ten meters away, the baby orangutan waited, face pressed to bars. Past it, two more cages held young ones curled together, orange fur blurring in the gloom.

Three lives—maybe four, if David's hands stayed steady and the rope let go in time.

But perfect wasn't something they could count on when every movement felt like moving through water.

The baby was awake, breath fogging the bars. Dark eyes followed David's every move, sharp, searching. He knelt, hands shaking, picking at the knots. The baby watched, silent and still—something almost human in its gaze, as if it understood.

"Wet rope," Rudi whispered, his fingers finding the knots. "Should come apart faster than ours did."

The rope went slick in his hands. Fever blurred his focus; every move was a battle. The fibers softened, but his grip slipped again and again.

Three minutes passed. Four.

Come on, David thought desperately. *Come on—*

The knot snapped. Wood creaked. The door swung wide, the sound huge in the dark. Both men froze, straining for any shout or step.

Nothing. Just the continued hum of generators and the soft sounds of sleeping animals.

The baby leapt to David, arms clinging tight around his neck, warm and wiry. It weighed almost nothing. Its damp fur smelled of earth and fear. Tiny fingers dug into his shirt, desperate for something lost.

The baby's weight was nothing—maybe six pounds. Less than his telephoto lens. It clung to him as if he were the mother it remembered, the one taken months ago. Its heartbeat against his ribs was rapid, bird-fast, trusting.

David's hands shook. He'd steadied cameras in Antarctic wind, kept lenses motionless during earthquakes. Now he couldn't hold still for a creature light as breath.

He limped to the forest edge, the baby pressed close. At the trees, he crouched low, coaxing it toward roots and leaves, whispering for instinct to wake.

The baby gripped his shirt, knuckles white. Then, with a shudder, it let go—something old and wild flickered in its eyes, memory older than cages.

It shuffled to the nearest tree, every step steadier. When it climbed, its body remembered—graceful, wild. David's heart squeezed as he watched it vanish upward.

Twenty feet up, the baby paused, glancing down—not for help, but in recognition. Then it melted into the leaves, swallowed by darkness.

One life—wild in the trees, a memory of freedom, no longer lost to cages.

"One," David whispered, the word carrying weight beyond simple mathematics.

"Second cage," Rudi replied, already moving back toward the camp. "Fast now. Twenty-five minutes left."

The next cage held twins, pressed together, eyes bright and wary. They remembered the forest—their shoulders twitched with hope, trauma not yet complete.

Rudi dug at the ropes, fingers quick and sure. David watched the shadows, heart pounding so loud it hurt. Every sound jumped—the rope splitting, animals breathing, the generator's growl.

Five minutes. The knots slipped free, each binding giving way under steady, practiced hands.

The twins bolted for the trees, pausing at the edge, glancing back. They scrambled up separate trunks, never straying far. The wild still lived between them.

Two more lives saved. Three total.

"Enough," Rudi whispered urgently, grabbing David's arm. "Twenty minutes gone. We go now while we still can."

A soft whimper pulled David to a third cage. Inside, a younger orangutan cowered, eyes haunted, the wild nearly erased by fear.

"One more," David said, already moving toward the cage despite Rudi's hand trying to restrain him.

"No time," Rudi hissed. "Guards coming soon. We saved three. That's enough."

"It's not enough." David kept moving, driven by a

momentum that felt larger than conscious decision. "Thirty seconds to open the cage. That's all we need."

"Thirty seconds we don't have." Rudi followed despite his objections. "This is stupid. This gets us killed."

"We're already dead," David replied, kneeling beside the third cage with hands that shook. "Might as well make it count."

This one didn't hope. Its eyes were wide, limbs stiff, every flinch telling a story of broken trust. Some cages crush more than bodies.

David fumbled, sweat and fever turning his hands clumsy. Wet rope held tight, tighter with every tug. Even simple acts were a struggle.

One minute passed. Two.

"David," Rudi breathed. "I hear something. Voices. Movement."

Distant sounds—footsteps approaching on patrol that were either early or they'd miscalculated time. Voices speaking in Indonesian, in a casual tone, suggesting routine rather than alarm, but a routine that would reveal them in seconds.

"Almost," David whispered, his hands working the knot that wouldn't give way. "Almost—"

"Leave it," Rudi hissed. "We go now or we die here."

The knot slipped. David gasped and yanked the cage open—just as flashlights cut across camp, searching.

The juvenile froze, eyes huge and body locked. The open door meant nothing—fear kept it rooted to the spot.

"Come," David whispered desperately, reaching for it. "Go. Run. Trees."

The orangutan remained motionless, its dark eyes wide with terror.

Shouts erupted across the camp—someone had noticed movement, or seen the open cages, or heard something that shouldn't exist in their controlled environment. Orders barked in Indonesian with authority that turned sleeping criminals into alert professionals within seconds.

"INTRUDERS! ESCAPING!"

Lights exploded across the camp, turning night into day in a single breath. Floodlights swept over empty cages, two escapees, and a breach worth millions exposed for all to see.

Terror broke its stillness. The juvenile lunged past David, scrambling for the trees, climbing fast. Old instincts woke up just as voices and flashlights closed in.

Four lives saved. Four endangered beings climbing through darkness toward freedom they'd otherwise never known.

"RUN!" Rudi grabbed David's arm, yanking him toward the forest edge.

They ran, but David's fever-weakened legs couldn't maintain the pace required to reach safety before pursuers closed the distance. Behind them, boots pounding wet ground, voices coordinating pursuit with military precision.

David's infected leg screamed with each impact. His vision fragmented into colors that shouldn't exist in nature. The adrenaline that had sustained him for thirty minutes was collapsing.

They ran, but only made it fifteen meters. Armed men melted from the shadows, snapping shut every way out.

David raised his hands in surrender, his chest heaving, feeling like he was drowning. His fever had spiked to a level that made standing difficult, and his entire body was shaking.

Rudi stood beside him, breathing hard but maintaining composure that suggested acceptance rather than surprise. They'd both known this outcome was likely. They'd chosen it anyway.

Harto emerged from the confusion, his expression carrying cold fury that spoke of professional embarrassment requiring severe response. The casual authority from yesterday had been replaced by genuine anger.

"You free animals?" he asked in English, his voice deadly quiet.

David considered lying, but the empty cages made deception pointless. "Yes."

Harto's smile was thin, nothing but calculation. "Foolish.

Animals are money. You've cost me, made me look weak. The people I answer to don't tolerate weakness."

He barked orders in rapid Indonesian, voice sharp with threat. David picked out enough words to know: this wasn't just punishment—they were being turned into an example.

They were marched back to the camp at gunpoint, David struggling to keep pace.

Through gaps in wooden structures, he could see guards searching the forest edge with flashlights, trying to recapture freed orangutans before they disappeared into terrain that favored arboreal species.

But the babies had vanished into the canopy's three-dimensional maze, climbing through branches toward freedom that professionals with weapons couldn't follow.

They were hauled into a bigger wooden cage—iron shackles waiting, wood thick and unforgiving. Metal bit into David's wrists, the sting a reminder that this cell wasn't meant for escape. Compared to this, their first cage felt almost gentle.

Through cracks in the walls came angry voices: the guards hadn't found the missing animals.

David sat beside Rudi, chains heavy between them. "Was it worth it?" he asked, voice low.

Rudi stared at the floor for a long time before answering. "Four lives free, not lost in cages. Three who might help their kind survive. Yes," he said softly. "It was worth it."

Four babies climbing through darkness toward freedom they'd otherwise never know.

Something settled in David—not pride, exactly. Certainty. Whatever came next, he'd finally done something that couldn't be photographed, archived, or displayed. Something that only mattered because he'd been willing to die for it.

Sarah wanted him to risk something real. Now he understood —it meant giving everything for creatures who'd never know his name, freeing lives that could never repay him.

Beyond the cage, the forest promised both freedom and

death. In the space between, courage found a home—unseen, unrecorded, but real.

Four baby orangutans are climbing through the darkness.

It was enough.

Even if no one else would ever know.

CHAPTER 7: FOUR LIVES FOR TWO

PART ONE: THE SILENCE

Day 2, 8:00 PM – Sydney, Australia.

Marcus Chen stared at his phone. Two days. David hadn't uploaded a backup in two days.

The backup notifications were a family joke. David's obsessive redundancy. Cloud bills that made Marcus groan. After Antarctica, David trusted nothing—not memory cards, not hard drives, not anything that could fail.

Two days of silence weren't a joke anymore.

Marcus scrolled through two years of backup notifications. Day after day, never a gap. Now, a forty-eight-hour silence screamed from the screen.

The last backup: "Day 1, 6:24 AM, Bukit Lawang, North Sumatra, Indonesia. 3 photos uploaded."

Nothing since. David never trusted technology, never left a single point of failure. A two-day gap meant something was wrong.

Marcus called, straight to voicemail.

He called again. Still nothing.

The unease crystallized into genuine concern. David was divorced, alone, traveling in remote Indonesian forests with a guide whose qualifications came from a website with mixed reviews. If something had gone wrong—if he'd gotten injured, or lost, or his equipment had failed—there would be no backup notifications because there would be no functioning phone to create them.

He opened David's cloud folder—shared after Antarctica. Three photos from two days ago: park gate, Rudi with the truck, forest at dawn. GPS points in every shot, all from the same morning.

Then nothing. Like David had vanished.

Marcus dialed the Australian Federal Police. A number he'd hoped to never use.

"AFP, how may I direct your call?"

"I need to report a potential missing person. Australian citizen, traveling in Indonesia, hasn't been heard from in two days."

The operator took notes, voice calm. Was this unusual? Marcus explained—David never missed a backup. No family, just Marcus.

"We'll contact the Australian Embassy in Jakarta," the operator said. "Can you give us his last GPS location?"

Marcus read out the coordinates. Bukit Lawang, North Sumatra. Park entrance.

"We'll start looking right away. If he calls, let us know."

The call ended. Marcus stared at his phone, hoping this was all a misunderstanding, that David just wanted a break from everything.

But Marcus knew better. He knew what Antarctica had done—why David never risked losing anything again.

Two days of silence were a warning Marcus couldn't ignore.

Part Two: Execution Morning

Day 3, 6:00 AM – Poaching Camp, North Sumatra

Dawn brought Harto.

Harto stood outside their cage as morning crept in. His face had the cold calm of a man set on his course.

"Four animals gone," he said flatly. "Searched all night. Nothing."

David felt grim satisfaction. Four babies gone, lost to the green where no gun could follow.

"You cost me forty thousand dollars. Maybe more." Harto's tone was flat, businesslike. "Worse, you make me look stupid to my bosses. They don't like stupid."

He paused, studying them like cattle before slaughter.

"Seven o'clock, you die. One hour." He checked his watch. "We make example. Show what happens when people fuck with my business. Then we move. New location, better security."

David's chest tightened, but fear felt far away. Fever, exhaustion, and a strange peace settled over him. He was ready for whatever came.

"Any requests?" Harto asked the question delivered with genuine curiosity rather than mockery.

"Let Rudi go," David said. "He's local—no one believes him anyway. Killing him does nothing."

Harto laughed, a real sound. "You beg for him, not yourself? Interesting." He shook his head. "No. He helped you. He chose this. Both die."

He snapped out orders in Indonesian. "One hour. Say your goodbyes."

He walked away. Morning sounds crept in—engines rumbling, workers shouting, animals crying from their cages.

Rudi sat beside him, both men shackled but finding comfort in shared imprisonment.

"I'm sorry," David whispered. "For your family. For what you're losing because of me."

"Not just you," Rudi replied quietly. "I stayed when I could run. I helped free animals when I could escape. My choice. My family."

"But Ratna and the girls—"

"They'll know their father died helping those who couldn't help themselves," Rudi said softly. "Better that than knowing I abandoned someone."

They sat in silence. The camp went on around them, business as usual, as if nothing was about to change.

"You found what you were looking for," Rudi said. "What your wife challenged you to find."

David heard Sarah's words—*When will you risk something that truly matters?* He'd found the answer here, at the edge of everything.

Four baby orangutans are climbing into the darkness. The truest picture—one no camera could capture—lived only in memory and in wild lives that went on.

"Yes," David said. "I found it."

～

Part Three: The Upload

Day 3, 6:30 AM – Sumatran Rainforest

The phone lay in leaf litter where David had dropped it two days ago, the screen cracked, but the electronics were functional, GPS active, the backup queue waiting for any cellular signal.

At 6:32 AM, atmospheric conditions and satellite positioning aligned—a brief window of signal penetration that David's paranoid configuration was designed to exploit.

One bar appeared. Then two.

The phone's backup system activated immediately, connecting with aggressive persistence. The upload queue contained sixty-three images—the poaching camp documentation, GPS-tagged evidence that international law enforcement had been seeking for years.

The upload began at 6:33 AM.

~

Day 3, 9:33 AM – Sydney, Australia

Marcus's phone began buzzing with notification after notification in rapid succession:

Cloud Backup Complete: 1 photo uploaded
 Location: Unknown, North Sumatra
 Timestamp: Day 2, 08:15 AM
 Cloud Backup Complete: 1 photo uploaded...

Marcus grabbed his phone, watching notifications flood in, disbelief turning to horror as he opened the first image.

A wooden cage. Baby orangutans pressed against bars. Tiny hands reaching through gaps.

Second image: Processing station. Equipment for systematic butchery. Stained tarps.

Third image: Armed guards with military-grade weapons.

Fourth image: Vehicles hidden under camouflage netting. License plates visible.

Sixty-three images documenting systematic slaughter with

GPS coordinates embedded in every file, pinpointing the operation's exact location.

Marcus's hands shook as he scrolled through the evidence, understanding immediately what David had found and why his backup notifications had stopped—operations like this couldn't afford witnesses.

He pulled up the metadata. GPS coordinates are approximately forty kilometers northeast of Bukit Lawang, deep in the primary rainforest.

"What the—?" he snatched the phone off the table.

He called AFP again; his voice was already rising when they picked up.

"This is Marcus Chen. I called last night about my cousin, David Chen, who is missing in Indonesia. I just received sixty-three backup photos from him—he's found a poaching operation. I have exact GPS coordinates. Armed guards, caged orangutans, trafficking evidence. He's in immediate danger."

"I'll transfer you to our emergency response coordinator immediately."

The next ten minutes were a blur—explaining the backup system, sending coordinates to AFP's secure server, watching as Australian authorities contacted the Indonesian military.

"Indonesian military is launching within the hour," the AFP coordinator told him. "Helicopter-based assault on those coordinates. If your cousin is there, they'll extract him."

If he's still alive, Marcus thought but didn't say.

The line went dead. Marcus sat in his Sydney apartment, praying that David's paranoid backup system—the obsessive redundancy Marcus had mocked constantly—would prove to be exactly the life-saving preparation David's Antarctica trauma had convinced him to maintain.

~

Part Four: The Price

. . .

Day 3, 7:00 AM – Execution Site

The birds had stopped calling. The forest felt emptied of its usual rhythm. Somewhere behind them, a spade struck dirt. It was the sound of a grave dug like a formality, as if death were a process already scheduled.

They came at seven o'clock exactly.

Three guards. Rifles ready. Expressions suggesting witness elimination were a routine operational necessity.

David's infected leg had swollen grotesquely overnight, red streaks reaching his groin. Each step sent white lightning through his nervous system, but adrenaline was enough to keep him walking.

They were marched past remaining cages—past orangutans pressing against bars, past processing stations, past the three empty cages where babies had been imprisoned until two humans chose courage over survival.

The camp was being dismantled. Whatever happened next, this operation would be gone by sunset, relocated to new coordinates.

But four baby orangutans were free. That knowledge sat in David's chest like ballast, heavy and permanent.

The execution site was a clearing at the forest's edge. A hole waited, raw and red. Six feet long. Three wide. Four deep. Earth piled in a neat mound beside it. Harto emerged from the tree line, now wearing clean tactical pants and a pressed shirt that seemed absurdly civilized for murder.

"Kneel."

David's legs folded automatically. The ground was wet against his knees. Beside him, Rudi knelt with the same mechanical compliance.

Harto drew his pistol. He aimed at David's forehead, hand steady.

David thought about Sarah's challenge—*When will you actually risk something that truly matters?* He'd found the answer in an Indonesian forest, kneeling beside a grave dug for his body.

Four baby orangutans climbing through the darkness.

That was enough.

David closed his eyes and waited for the sound that would end everything.

Instead, he heard something else. Distant but unmistakable—a sound that didn't belong in this forest, this moment, this execution.

The rhythmic thump of helicopter rotors. Multiple helicopters. Coming fast.

David's eyes opened. Harto had frozen, his weapon still raised, but his attention diverted to the approaching sound growing louder with each second.

"Impossible," Harto breathed. "How—"

Voices erupted across the camp behind them. Shouts in Indonesian—alarm, confusion, realization that their remote location had been compromised.

The helicopter sounds grew louder. Multiple aircraft are approaching from different directions, executing a coordinated military assault with precision.

Harto's gaze flicked from his prisoners to the helicopters closing in. If he killed them now, the military would come for him as a murderer. If he didn't, he might still have a chance to run.

He lowered his weapon and ran, choosing survival over revenge.

Guards scattered throughout the camp, their systematic security collapsing under unexpected tactical assault. The professional operation that had relied on remoteness was discovering that isolation worked both ways.

Through the trees, David could see the first helicopter descending below canopy level, rotors creating a downdraft that bent trees and scattered leaf litter. Military markings. The Indonesian Air Force is conducting a coordinated, precision assault, citing exact coordinates and detailed intelligence.

How? His fevered brain struggled to understand. Then he remembered: the phone. His cracked phone with a paranoid backup system, dropped during the chase, but still functional, still trying to upload, still embedding GPS coordinates.

The paranoia that seemed excessive in civilization had just saved their lives.

More helicopters appeared, surrounding the camp with overwhelming force. Rappelling soldiers in tactical gear descended, weapons trained, movements coordinated.

"DOWN!" someone shouted through the loudspeaker. "INDONESIAN MILITARY. DROP YOUR WEAPONS. THIS FACILITY IS SURROUNDED."

David and Rudi remained kneeling beside the grave dug for their bodies, understanding they'd just witnessed the narrowest escape from execution that human experience allowed.

Four baby orangutans are free in the forest.

And two humans who'd chosen principle over survival, discovering that sometimes—against all probability—courage was rewarded with outcomes that rational calculation suggested were impossible.

The helicopters thundered overhead, and David Chen began to understand that his paranoid preparation had proven to be exactly the salvation his Antarctica trauma had convinced him to maintain.

Marcus had noticed. Marcus had acted. The backup system had uploaded.

And military rescue had arrived exactly in time.

CHAPTER 8: THE RESCUE

Day 3, 7:00 AM—The assault

The helicopter descended through the canopy. Rotor wash bent trees, sent leaves spinning, turned the clearing into a storm of green confetti. David watched from his knees, beside the grave meant for him. Survival and death split by seconds—none of them his to choose.

Indonesian flags flashed on uniforms. Soldiers slid down ropes, a single organism in motion. This was no rescue; it was an assault. Every movement radiated discipline.

This was no accident. Every movement coordinated. Every position calculated. Someone had given them the exact coordinates.

"INDONESIAN MILITARY!" The voice thundered over the camp. "DROP YOUR WEAPONS! YOU'RE SURROUNDED!"

Gunfire erupted from every direction. Rifle cracks tangled with the thunder of rotors. David's fevered mind reeled—sound, heat, violence closing in from all sides.

Harto disappeared into the jungle, execution abandoned. A

few guards bolted after him, dissolving into the green. The rest stood paralyzed, hands raised, faces drained of color. To resist now was to die.

Three helicopters circled in. The forest that had trapped him now blocked escape for everyone. Boots hit the ground—soldiers moved with purpose, weapons ready.

Professional. Overwhelming. The kind of force poachers feared most.

"Two civilians at the grave site!" a soldier shouted in English. "Immediate danger!"

Boots thundered closer. David tried to stand, but his legs failed him. Shackles bit his wrists. His body felt distant, numb with fever and shock. Only the soldiers were real, rushing in to save him by the narrowest margin.

Three soldiers knelt by them, weapons ready but pointed down. One checked David's pulse, hands steady and sure.

"Australian?" the soldier asked, voice clipped.

"Yes," David rasped.

"David Chen?"

They knew his name. That meant AFP was involved, Marcus's frantic calls, intelligence working overtime—turning a missing-person case into a military rescue in just thirty-six hours. His backup system had done more than upload evidence; it had delivered the coordinates that brought the soldiers here.

"Medic!" the soldier yelled. "Priority—sepsis! Immediate evac!"

Hands pried at his shackles. Bolt cutters snapped them off. Raw skin burned as blood rushed back to his fingers.

Rudi's shackles fell too. He looked spent, eyes wide with relief and disbelief.

Soldiers swept the camp, moving as teams. Buildings cleared, criminals cuffed, evidence bagged. This was no first rescue.

The orangutans wailed above the noise. Wildlife handlers moved in—different uniforms, gentle hands. This operation had been planned for everyone, animal and human.

"Can you walk?" the medic asked. He already knew the answer.

"Don't think so."

"Stretcher! On the bird now!" the medic barked. "He needs antibiotics, fast."

The words should have scared David. But fever made everything far away. Death from infection or execution—did it matter?

Two soldiers lifted him onto a stretcher, straps snug. Canvas felt impossibly soft after days on wood and dirt. Comfort, finally, but almost too late.

Rudi shuffled beside him, a soldier at his arm. He looked ready to collapse.

"You did good," David told his guide, the words requiring more effort than they should have.

"We both did," Rudi replied. "Four babies free. That matters."

"It matters," David whispered. The world broke into fever and color as they carried him away.

Evacuation was a blur—straps, hands, IV needles. David was loaded into the helicopter. Rudi climbed in beside him. Comfort, even now.

They had survived—together. Chosen what was right, not what was safe. Found courage neither expected.

Through the helicopter door, David saw the camp sprawling below—bigger than he'd known. Not local poachers. This was industry. Organized extinction on a scale he'd never imagined.

The helicopter veered toward Medan. The green canopy unfurled beneath them. The jungle that nearly claimed him now protected the lives he'd fought to save.

"Stay with me," the medic said, noting David's unfocused gaze with professional concern. "Don't check out yet. We're twenty minutes from hospital."

David tried to speak, but nothing came out. Fever scorched through him, thoughts dissolving into fog, effort evaporating. What felt manageable yesterday now raged wild—his body losing ground, infection closing in.

Rudi's hand gripped his. Three days ago, strangers. Now, brothers—bound by terror, courage, and the will to survive.

The helicopter's medical bay bristled with equipment David's fevered mind couldn't name—monitors blinking unreadable numbers, IV bags dripping into his failing veins, instruments ready for emergencies he could barely imagine.

"Pressure dropping," someone said. "Thready pulse. More fluids."

David felt hands adjusting tubes, tugging wires, pressure building in his veins. His body floated, passive, as medicine surged in. Survival was no longer his to command—his life belonged to others now.

Irony struck. Years spent behind a camera, shielded from danger. Now he was the story—the suffering, the crisis. No lens left to hide behind.

Sarah would understand. He had become someone worth being—someone who risked everything, reward or not.

The helicopter dipped toward Medan. City lights swelled below. Civilization waited—the world he'd left behind, forever changed by the jungle's secrets.

"Landing in two minutes," the pilot announced. "Medical team standing by."

The helicopter landed on the hospital roof, medical teams surging forward in a storm of organized chaos. David moved from helicopter to gurney to elevator to emergency room in a blur— one seamless rush, not separate moments.

Fluorescent lights blinded him after days of green twilight. White walls pulsed and breathed. The sharp tang of antiseptic burned his nostrils—jungle damp replaced by chemicals that promised sterility but felt like violence. Voices snapped in rapid Indonesian and clipped English, words fracturing into meaningless sound. Hands sliced away his filthy clothes, exposing wounds so dire that even seasoned professionals gasped.

"Severe cellulitis with probable septicemia," someone said with the clinical detachment that came from extensive emergency experience. "Get him on broad-spectrum antibiotics immediately. I want cultures, CBC, metabolic panel, and get the infectious disease team down here stat."

David tried to follow the chaos, but his fever scattered his thoughts. Faces flickered in and out. Voices barked orders he couldn't grasp. Needles stabbed his skin again and again, interventions piling up faster than he could count.

Somewhere in the controlled chaos, Rudi's voice penetrated the medical activity: "He saved animals. He chose courage over survival. Please—help him."

"We're doing everything we can," someone replied with the kind reassurance medical professionals offered families who needed hope more than clinical assessment.

Then darkness swept in—not death, but the deep unconsciousness that comes when body and mind surrender, shutting down to avoid total collapse.

David Chen's last thought was of four baby orangutans climbing through the night forest, tiny hands grasping branches with wisdom captivity had buried but never erased.

He'd done something worth doing.

If this was the end—on a Medan hospital bed, body locked in battle with invisible enemies—at least he had become someone worth remembering.

Someone who'd risked everything that mattered.

Someone worthy of Rudi's courage, of the sacrifices they both made, of the lives they saved against all odds and with so little time.

The darkness deepened, drawing him under with the slow certainty of a tide claiming sand. David let go, no longer resisting the surrender his body craved.

Somewhere between the trees and the hospital roof, consciousness thinned. He felt himself drift — between forest and fluorescent light, between worlds that would never touch again.

CHAPTER 9: AFTERMATH

REGIONAL HOSPITAL, MEDAN—DAY 9, 2:00 PM

David woke to white walls and the insistent beep of machines tracking numbers he couldn't name. His mouth tasted like metal and old blood.

For a moment, nothing made sense. Memory broke into shards—rotor blades, green canopy, a grave in the dirt, hands on iron shackles.

His leg ached. Dull, not the fire he'd remembered. Bandages circled his wrists, white against torn skin. The IV dripped into his arm. Each drop louder than the clock. Each one proved he was still here.

How long had he been here?

"You're awake." The voice came from beside his bed—a nurse who'd apparently been monitoring him with the patient attention that characterized professional medical care. "Good. Dr. Anwar will want to examine you."

"How long?" David's voice emerged as a rough whisper, his throat raw from intubation he didn't remember.

"Three days unconscious. Three more days sedated while we

fought the infection." The nurse checked his IV line with practiced efficiency. "You've been very sick, Mr. Chen. Sepsis, organ stress, severe dehydration. We weren't certain you'd pull through."

Six days. Almost a week since the rescue. Since Harto raised the pistol. Since helicopters cut through the trees and brought salvation he hadn't dared imagine.

"Rudi?" David asked the question, carrying weight beyond a simple inquiry about his guide's health.

"Mr. Santoso is fine. Exhausted, dehydrated, but no serious infection. He's been here every day, waiting for you to wake up. His wife and daughters came yesterday." The nurse smiled. "He's a very loyal friend."

Friend. Not a guide. Not the client. Not business. Just a friend.

The door opened. Dr. Anwar entered. Steady hands. Eyes that had seen too many tourists underestimate the jungle. She checked his leg, fingers gentle over the incision where surgeons had cut away infection.

"The cellulitis had progressed to necrotizing fasciitis," she explained, her English clinical but clear. "We had to debride significant tissue from your calf. You'll have scarring, probably some permanent weakness. But you'll keep the leg, which was uncertain when you arrived."

He listened. Calm. He'd made peace with dying days ago. The leg was a bonus. Something he hadn't counted on.

"You're very lucky," Dr. Anwar continued. "Twelve more hours without treatment and we'd be discussing amputation or systemic failure. The military medics who stabilized you during transport deserve significant credit."

"When can I leave?"

"Another week, minimum. Possibly two depending on how the wound heals. The infection is controlled but not eliminated. You'll need IV antibiotics for several more days, then oral medications for weeks after discharge."

She made notes on his chart with the systematic attention that suggested she'd delivered similar lectures to foolish tourists before. "You should know—there are people waiting to speak with you. Indonesian police, Australian Federal Police, and wildlife investigators. They've been patient, but now that you're conscious..." She paused. "Are you ready for visitors?"

David nodded. The photos had blown things open. Now they wanted his words to finish the job.

Inspector Sari from the Indonesian National Police arrived thirty minutes later, carrying a tablet and the kind of focused intensity that suggested she'd been waiting days for this conversation.

"Mr. Chen." She pulled a chair close to his bed. "I'm glad you're recovering. What you did was very brave. Also very stupid, but mostly brave."

David appreciated the honesty more than diplomatic platitudes. "The criminals?"

"Fourteen arrests at the camp," Inspector Sari said, pulling up images on her tablet. "Harto Sungkar and thirteen of his operation—guards, processing workers, logistics coordinators. Your phone's automatic backup gave us exact GPS coordinates. Military assault was launched within hours."

She showed him brief footage of helicopters descending through the forest canopy, soldiers securing the camp with tactical precision.

"Harto was captured six hours after the initial raid," she continued. "He fled into the forest, but tracking units located him. He's currently in custody awaiting trial on multiple charges: trafficking endangered species, attempted murder, operating a criminal enterprise, and money laundering. The case will take months to build, but with your evidence, prosecutors are confident of a conviction. He's looking at twenty years minimum if found guilty."

Something loosened in his chest. Harto was caught. Justice, finally, was moving.

"The animals?" David asked.

"Twenty-eight orangutans recovered from the facility," Inspector Sari said. "Also, fifteen gibbons, eight sun bears, and over a hundred exotic birds. All receiving veterinary care. Some will be rehabilitated and released. Others are too traumatized— they'll go to sanctuaries."

Twenty-eight orangutans. Each one is a thread holding together a species with only 14,000 left.

"And the four we freed?" David asked, the question carrying weight beyond simple curiosity.

Inspector Sari's expression softened. "Wildlife biologists have been monitoring the release area with motion-activated cameras. Three confirmed survivors—building nests, foraging successfully, showing natural behaviors." She pulled up grainy footage of a young orangutan moving through branches with increasing confidence. "This one we're very confident about. Strong adaptation."

A second clip showed two orangutans traveling together—the twins. "These two maintained their social bond. Both are adapting well."

"The fourth?"

Inspector Sari admitted. "The fourth didn't make it. Found dead two weeks after release. Stress from captivity, we think."

David's hand moved to his leg, pressing the scar through his pants. One life lost. Three saved. The math wasn't clean, but it was honest. Better than four lives dying in cages while he did nothing.

"Your documentation was crucial," Inspector Sari continued. "The GPS coordinates allowed immediate response. Your images provide evidence for prosecution." She pulled up several of David's photos—baby orangutans pressed against bars, processing stations, armed guards. "These have been shared with INTERPOL and wildlife enforcement agencies. Your work under such dangerous circumstances is now helping investigators identify similar operations elsewhere."

His worst images. Blurry, snapped on the run. Those were the ones making a difference. Not just awareness. Real change.

"What happens now?" David asked.

"For you? Heal, give formal testimony when you're strong enough, then go home." Inspector Sari stood. "For Harto? Prosecution, asset seizure, dismantling everything he built. Your courage cost him everything."

After she left, David stared at the ceiling. Twenty-eight animals rescued. Fourteen arrests. A ring is broken. The numbers filled the room. Still not enough.

But the fourth orangutan was missing. Forests kept falling. Other traffickers would step in. Extinction pressed closer. Bigger than any arrest. Bigger than him.

The work mattered. It still wasn't enough.

The door opened again—Rudi this time, accompanied by a woman David assumed was his wife Ratna and two small girls who watched him with the frank curiosity of children trying to understand why their father's tourist client was in a hospital bed covered in bandages.

"You're awake," Rudi said, his relief evident. "We've been waiting."

"Inspector Sari told me everything," David replied. "Three babies surviving in the forest. Harto captured. Fourteen arrests."

"Yes." Rudi settled into the chair beside the bed while his daughters climbed onto their mother's lap. "The babies are free because we chose courage. The operation shut down because your paranoid backup system worked. Not bad for three days in forest."

David smiled despite his exhaustion. "Not bad for a stupid tourist and his guide."

"Not guide," Rudi corrected gently. "Partner. Friend. Someone who'll tell this story to his daughters when they're old enough to understand what their father did when need courage."

Ratna spoke for the first time, her English careful but clear. "Thank you for bringing my husband home."

"He saved me," David replied, remembering those crucial

moments when Rudi could have fled but instead knelt to gather scattered camera equipment.

The younger daughter—Sinta, David remembered from Rudi's descriptions—spoke in Indonesian to her mother, who translated: "She wants to know if the baby orangutans are happy now."

David thought about the motion-activated camera footage—young orangutans building nests, foraging independently, remembering what captivity had tried to erase. The fourth one hadn't survived. Three lives saved. One lost. "Yes," he said. "I think they're happy."

That evening, alone in his hospital room, David's phone finally powered on. Recovered from the forest. Returned in a plastic evidence bag. The cracked screen glowed. Missed calls. Messages. Voicemails he couldn't face yet.

He scrolled past most of them, looking for one name.

Marcus had called seventeen times. The most recent message, sent just that morning: "They told me you're going to make it. Call when you can. Your paranoia saved your life, mate. Never letting you forget that."

David smiled and typed a response: "Paranoia pays off. Antarctica trauma for the win. Thanks for noticing when the backups stopped."

The response came within seconds: "That's what family does. Now get better and come home. You owe me dinner and the full story."

Further down the list: Sarah.

Just one message, sent two days ago when news of the rescue had apparently reached Australian media: "Saw the reports. You finally found what you were looking for. Proud of you. Come home safe."

Proud. The same word Sari used. The same look Rudi gave him when he talked about courage.

Eight years dodging the risks Sarah wanted him to face. Always behind the camera. Never in the fight. Comfort over commitment. Awareness instead of action. No wonder the marriage cracked.

But in the forest, kneeling by his own grave, he learned what commitment meant. Not pretty photos. Not awards. Not safe donations. Just risking everything for something bigger than himself. Finally.

He typed a response to Sarah: "Found it. Almost died finding it. But worth it. Thank you for pushing me to look."

Message delivered. Not read. Sarah was probably at her desk, juggling clients, living a life far from this hospital bed. They wouldn't get back together. The split ran deeper than fear. Deeper than risk. They wanted different things.

Evening light faded through the window. Traffic and construction bled in. The city moved on, uncaring. David understood: the forest had changed him. What came next would be different.

He couldn't go back to safe jobs, shooting crises from a distance. Couldn't take assignments for the portfolio, not the cause. Couldn't keep hiding behind work Sarah had called out as avoidance.

The work had to matter. Had to cost something. Had to help more than just his resume.

Three baby orangutans are alive in the forest because they'd chosen courage over comfort. Twenty-eight animals are safe because his paranoia had worked.

That was the new standard. Not perfection. Three survivors meant one lost. Twenty-eight rescued meant thousands are still dying. But it was a contribution, not just watching.

His leg throbbed, pain breaking through the meds. Courage had a price. The scar would stay, proof of choices that couldn't be erased.

But he kept the leg. Kept his life.

That was enough.

That was everything.

Night shift started. Nurses checked vitals, adjusted meds, and faces unreadable. They'd seen tourists like him before. David let them work. Grateful. Alive.

Second chance. Time to build something real. The forest had stripped away comfort, leaving only what mattered.

The next assignment would be harder. No dramatic rescue. No military helicopters. Just months of patient documentation that might lead to nothing.

But he'd do it anyway. That was the difference.

He'd been tested. Found courage he didn't know he had, pulled out by Rudi's loyalty and four desperate orangutans.

The forest showed him who he was when comfort vanished.

Now he had to hold onto that person, even when comfort crept back in.

The work was just beginning.

For the first time since his marriage ended, David felt ready for whatever came next.

CHAPTER 10: PROOF OF LIFE

SIX MONTHS LATER—GUNUNG LEUSER NATIONAL PARK, North Sumatra

Leaves glistened with last night's rain. David's boots pressed into mud that felt different—though whether the forest had changed or he had was impossible to say.

David pushed through tangled undergrowth. Rudi kept pace, both men traveling light. Dr. Sarah Pritchard led, boots sure, eyes scanning for a sign. David's leg throbbed from the climb. Scar tissue pulled tight with each step. The ache was earned.

His camera hung around his neck, lighter than the equipment he'd carried six months ago. One body, one lens, focusing on documentation that mattered rather than gear that impressed. The photographs he was creating now served conservation purposes rather than aesthetic achievement, evidence rather than art.

Sometimes, when light cut through the canopy just right, evidence and art blurred. For a moment, the difference vanished.

"The monitoring station is just ahead," Dr. Pritchard said, ducking under a low branch. "We've been tracking the three individuals you freed for the past six months. The data is... remarkable, actually."

David met Rudi's eyes. Six months of waiting. Had they saved lives, or just sent three broken animals to die slowly in a forest they barely remembered?

"All three?" David asked, not quite daring to hope.

"You'll see." Dr. Pritchard smiled, the expression carrying professional satisfaction mixed with something deeper. "We don't usually get to show people the direct results of their courage. This is special."

A wooden platform circled an ancient tree. Cameras watched the canopy. Solar panels blinked green. Dr. Pritchard tapped her tablet. Footage flickered—months of orangutan lives compressed into minutes. David leaned in, hungry for answers.

"Subject One," Dr. Pritchard began, showing footage of the first baby they'd freed—the eighteen-month-old who'd been watching them through cage bars, whose intelligent eyes had seemed to understand rescue was coming. "Initial observations showed expected difficulty with foraging—choosing wrong fruits, inefficient nest construction, excessive ground travel suggesting incomplete understanding of arboreal safety."

The screen showed a young orangutan, clumsy in the branches. Wrong fruit. Nests that collapsed. Movements wild-born animals never made.

"But look at this." Dr. Pritchard scrolled forward three months. "Complete behavioral adaptation. Proper food selection, efficient travel through the canopy, and nest construction that matches wild-born individuals of similar age. This animal remembered everything it needed to survive. It just needed time to reaccess that knowledge."

Now the orangutan moved with purpose. Branch to branch, sure-footed. Fingers tested fruit, picked only the ripe. Nests held through the rain. Wild memory, awake again.

"It's thriving," Dr. Pritchard said simply. "Full wild adaptation. This individual will contribute to the breeding population once it reaches maturity."

One life back where it belonged. One survivor, future written in muscle and bone. The forest had room for one more.

"Subjects Two and Three," Dr. Pritchard continued, pulling up footage of the twins who'd fled together during the rescue. "Social bond maintained throughout the rehabilitation period. They've actually taught each other—one figured out certain foraging techniques faster, the other was better at nest construction. They observed and learned from each other, demonstrating exactly the kind of cultural transmission we see in wild populations."

Two juveniles moved through the forest together. No desperate clinging now. They shared food, played, and learned. Close enough for safety, free enough to grow.

"Both showing excellent wild adaptation," Dr. Pritchard confirmed. "Their social bond is actually an advantage—mutual support during what should have been an impossibly difficult transition from captivity to freedom."

Three more lives. Three more individuals whose genetics would contribute to species survival.

David felt something loosen in his chest that had been tight for six months—the uncertainty about whether their desperate rescue had accomplished anything beyond making themselves feel better about horrors they'd witnessed.

Three for three. All alive. All learning the forest again.

"You should know," Dr. Pritchard said, "this outcome is extremely unusual. Most rehabilitation programs take years of careful intervention. You released traumatized juveniles into an uncontrolled environment with no preparation, no support system, and no gradual reintroduction. By every standard protocol, they should have died within weeks."

She paused. Studied them. Reckless, by any standard. But the evidence spoke for itself.

"But they didn't die. They thrived. And we're still trying to understand why your approach worked when careful methodology often fails. Current theory is that the trauma of captivity was brief enough that species memory remained accessible—captivity hadn't overwritten their inherited knowledge, just temporarily suppressed it. Freedom was enough to let that knowledge resurface."

"Or maybe they were just ready," Rudi said quietly. "Maybe some beings are stronger than we think."

Dr. Pritchard nodded. "Maybe. Either way, you gave them a chance they wouldn't have had. Three endangered individuals contributing to the wild population because two humans chose courage over calculated survival."

She pulled up additional data—weight gain suggesting proper nutrition, ranging patterns indicating territorial establishment, and social interactions with other wild orangutans demonstrating successful integration into existing populations. Every metric showed successful rehabilitation that defied professional expectations.

"The twenty-eight rescued from the camp are doing well, too," Dr. Pritchard added, anticipating the question. Twelve have been released after careful rehabilitation. Eight more will be released next year. Eight are too traumatized for full wild release—they'll live in semi-wild sanctuary conditions. All alive, all receiving care they need."

Twenty-eight lives pulled from cages. Not all would return to the wild. Some would breed, some would teach, and all would prove recovery was possible if someone intervened.

"What about Harto?" David asked, the name still carrying weight despite six months of distance.

"Trial begins next month," Dr. Pritchard replied. "Prosecutors are using your documentation as primary evidence. International trafficking charges, attempted murder, and operating a criminal enterprise. They're seeking maximum sentences—twenty to thirty years. Your photographs made the case undefendable."

Justice, not theory. Real consequences. No more easy escapes.

That evening, after Dr. Pritchard disappeared into the glow of her research station, David and Rudi sat at the edge of the forest. Dusk slid between the trees, painting the leaves in deep blues and golds. The jungle's breath was thick with earth and distant bird calls. Six months ago, this place had felt like a living threat—every shadow a warning. Now, the air still tingled with danger, but something had changed. The wild pressed close, rough and restless, but no longer a predator waiting to swallow them whole.

"You've changed," Rudi observed, his English even more fluent after months of partnership on various conservation projects. "Six months ago, you were a tourist with expensive cameras. Now you're something else."

"What am I now?" David asked, genuinely curious about how his transformation appeared to someone who'd witnessed both versions.

"Someone who found work worth dying for," Rudi replied. "And having found it, chose to keep living so the work could continue."

The observation was accurate in ways that made David uncomfortable. He had changed—not just in obvious ways like the permanent limp and the scar tissue marking his leg, but in a fundamental approach to how he spent his time and what he considered meaningful.

The past six months had been the busiest and most fulfilling of his professional life. Working with conservation organizations across Southeast Asia, documenting anti-poaching operations and rehabilitation efforts, creating evidence that supported prosecution and funding rather than just raising awareness. The partnership with Rudi had evolved into something neither man had anticipated—an equal collaboration between someone who knew forests and someone who knew documentation, cultural knowledge meeting technical capability in ways that accomplished more than either could achieve alone.

The pay was worse. The risk is higher. No awards. No gallery shows. But the work mattered. Impact, not distance.

"What do you tell your daughters?" David asked. "About what we did here?"

"I tell them their father learned that some things are worth risking everything for," Rudi replied. "That courage isn't absence of fear—it's choosing principle despite fear. That three baby orangutans are alive because two scared men decided being brave was more important than being safe."

He paused, watching evening light fade through trees that had witnessed human drama but remained fundamentally indifferent to outcomes that mattered desperately to the small creatures navigating their massive trunks.

"I tell them that their father died a little bit in that forest," Rudi continued. "The version who accepted comfortable employment serving tourists who wanted adventure without risk. And someone better emerged—someone who understood that meaningful work requires meaningful sacrifice."

David thought about Sarah's challenge—*When will you actually risk something that truly matters?*—and realized he was finally living the answer. Six months of work that scared him, that required competence he was still developing, that served outcomes extending far beyond his own portfolio or career trajectory.

He'd turned down three magazine assignments that would have paid well and required minimal risk. Had accepted projects in Myanmar, Cambodia, and Indonesian Papua that paid barely enough to cover expenses and required entering circumstances where personal safety couldn't be guaranteed. Had created documentation that would never appear in galleries but would support prosecutions, funding applications, and policy changes that actually protected endangered species rather than just commemorating their extinction.

Photography had changed for him. The camera was no longer a shield. Now it was a tool. Evidence, not distance.

"My mother asked if I was trying to die," David said, remembering a difficult conversation with Margaret Chen, who'd been horrified by news of his near-execution and concerned about the dangerous work he'd accepted afterward. "She said I survived once by luck and seemed determined to tempt fate until my luck ran out."

"What did you tell her?"

"That I was trying to live," David replied. "Really live, for the first time since Antarctica taught me how easily documentation can be lost and how much it matters to create backup systems protecting work from simple technology failure."

Antarctica had made him paranoid. That paranoia saved him. Backup files were uploaded while he bled out. Marcus noticed when the uploads stopped. The raid came because GPS data survived, even when he didn't.

Obsession looked like paranoia, until it didn't. Until it saved your life.

"Sarah was right about everything," David continued, needing to speak the truth that had taken six months to understand fully. "I spent eight years avoiding risk that mattered, maintaining a safe distance from crises I documented, choosing experiences that served my growth without requiring sacrifice that might damage my comfort. She saw through the sophisticated avoidance I'd dressed up as professional dedication."

"And now?" Rudi asked.

"Now I choose projects that scare me," David said. "Work where success isn't guaranteed and failure might mean physical danger or financial loss, or discovering I'm not as competent as comfortable assignments let me believe. Work where outcomes matter more than whether I survive to document them."

He pulled out his phone—new model since the cracked one that had saved his life was now preserved in evidence bags waiting for Harto's trial—and scrolled to a message from John sent that morning:

New assignment offer from National Geographic. Three months documenting Arctic climate research. Great pay, minimal danger, perfect for your portfolio. Should I tell them you're interested?

David had stared at that message for an hour, tempted by safety, professional prestige, and work that wouldn't require courage beyond enduring cold weather and occasional equipment failure.

Then he'd replied: *Thanks, but committed to anti-poaching work through the end of the year. Recommend James Morrison—he'd be perfect for the Arctic assignment.*

He chose meaning. Risk. Work that could kill him, not just pad a resume.

"You're building something," Rudi observed. "Not just taking photographs—building a documentation system that serves justice rather than just awareness. Building partnerships between local knowledge and technical capability. Building evidence that actually changes outcomes."

Rudi was right. David had built more than projects. Training programs. Partnerships. Funding for work that mattered. He was building something that would last. Whether he retired or vanished in the forest, the work would go on.

"The freed babies," David said, returning to the footage Dr. Pritchard had shown them. "They're the measure. If those three are thriving, then everything we risked was justified. If they'd died, then courage without competence is just expensive stupidity."

"But they didn't die," Rudi replied. "They're thriving. Which means our courage accomplished something beyond making ourselves feel brave. We gave three endangered beings the chance to contribute to their species' survival. That matters more than whether we were competent or lucky or blessed by forest spirits who occasionally favor fools."

Evening faded fast. Dusk dropped like a curtain. Insects started up, then frogs, then birds. The forest sang a song older than humans. It would keep singing, no matter what people did.

"What's next for you?" David asked Rudi, knowing his partner had received offers from multiple conservation organizations, impressed by his combination of local knowledge and demonstrated bravery under impossible circumstances.

"Wildlife Conservation International wants me to coordinate anti-poaching operations across North Sumatra," Rudi said. "Good salary, meaningful work, dangerous enough that Ratna alternates between pride and terror about what might happen to me. But the work matters. Really matters. And having tasted work that matters..." He paused. "I can't go back to guiding tourists who want adventure without risk."

"We're ruined for normal employment," David observed.

"Completely ruined," Rudi agreed. "But I'd rather be ruined doing work worth dying for than comfortable doing work that doesn't matter beyond paying bills."

They sat in silence as darkness settled. The forest had nearly killed them. Instead, it had given them purpose.

Twenty-eight orangutans, somewhere, are learning again. Fourteen criminals await trial. The evidence mattered now.

Above them, the jungle rustled. Three young orangutans moved through branches, invisible but present. Somewhere in the dark, a branch bent under weight, then sprang back.

David looked up, listening.

He thought of Sarah watching the story she'd once asked him to risk for something real.

He knew now that witnessing wasn't the same as staying.

Then he turned toward the trees.

～

AFTER THE FOREST

By the time you reach this page, you've seen what this story asks of its characters.

Blood & Leaves is not about adventure, heroism, or the romance of wild places. It is about what happens when witnessing is no longer enough—when seeing harm creates a responsibility that cannot be set aside without consequence.

Some readers will finish this book angry.

Some unsettled.

Some quietly changed by the weight of what was seen, and what was done.

If this story stayed with you—if it raised questions about complicity, courage, or the cost of choosing to act—I would appreciate you sharing a brief, honest Amazon review. Not a summary, but your response to the experience of reading it: what disturbed you, what felt real, what lingered after the final page.

Your reflection helps other readers decide whether this is a story they are willing to face.

Thank you for reading.

And for staying with what could not be unseen.

AUTHOR'S NOTE

This story began in the green hush of the Sumatran rainforest, where I once got lost with a guide who knew less than he claimed.

What you've just read is fiction. David Chen is invented. The poaching operation is fabricated. The military rescue never happened. But my experience of being lost in that forest—the fear, the physical breakdown, the way the jungle strips away everything except the question of who you are when comfort disappears—that parallels the story you've just read. I went there to see orangutans in the wild, just like David. I didn't find them—or rather, I found something else: the limits of my own preparation, and the measure of another man's character. When leg cramps finally dragged me down and I couldn't walk anymore, my guide could have saved himself. He could have left me there and gone for help. Instead, he stayed. Like Rudi in this story, he chose loyalty over survival, putting himself at risk when the rational choice was to run. That moment—when I understood what it meant for someone to choose principle over safety—changed everything. And the realization I'd been running from myself rather than toward anything real? That was true too.

The poaching operation David stumbles upon is fictional, but the threats facing Sumatran orangutans are devastatingly real. Fewer than 14,000 remain in fragmented forest reserves, their habitat destroyed by palm oil plantations and illegal logging at rates that could lead to extinction within our lifetimes. Wildlife trafficking networks operate with industrial efficiency across Southeast Asia, treating endangered species as profitable inventory in markets worth millions of dollars annually.

I've tried to honor the complexity of these issues without oversimplifying the cultural and economic pressures that drive both conservation and exploitation. The Indonesian characters in this story—particularly Rudi Santoso—represent the local knowledge and courage that make genuine conservation possible, rather than the Western savior narratives that too often dominate environmental storytelling.

This is a story of collision: comfort meeting the sharp edge of reality, romance dissolving in the sweat and ache of real fear. It is about the moment you discover what you would carry through the dark, and what you would leave behind.

The orangutans are real. The threats are real. The choice between comfort and courage is real.

I hope these pages do justice to the ones who cannot speak for themselves, and to those who guard them—quietly, at great cost, with no audience but the trees. Some lives are worth saving, even if no one is watching.

To the forests that reveal who we really are.

To the creatures who can't speak for themselves.

To everyone willing to risk everything for principles that matter more than personal safety.

This story is for you.

~

A Request from the Author

. . .

If this story moved you, challenged you, or made you think differently about courage and conservation, I'd be deeply grateful if you'd take a moment to share your thoughts.

Reader reviews—whether a few sentences or detailed reflections—help other readers discover stories that might resonate with them. Your honest feedback makes it possible for independent stories like this one to find their audience.

What did the journey mean to you? Did David and Rudi's choices feel authentic? Did the forest come alive in your imagination?

I read every review and truly value your perspective.

Thank you for spending your time in the Sumatran rainforest with these characters. Thank you for caring about stories that ask what we're willing to risk for what we believe matters.

—Sage Kane